D0256425

For Jill, Coco, Honey, Bonnie, Belle and Polly Grey – **M.S.**

For Millie, Candy
and everyone's canine pals – **S.C.**

BLOOMSBURY CHILDREN'S BOOKS
Bloomsbury Publishing Plc
50 Bedford Square, London, WC1B 3DP, UK
29 Earlsfort Terrace, Dublin 2, Ireland

BLOOMSBURY, BLOOMSBURY CHILDREN'S BOOKS and the Diana logo
are trademarks of Bloomsbury Publishing Plc

First published in Great Britain 2022 by Bloomsbury Publishing Plc

A catalogue record for this book is available from the British Library

ISBN 978 1 4088 7612 1 (HB)
ISBN 978 1 4088 7611 4 (PB)
ISBN 978 1 4088 7613 8 (eBook)

1 3 5 7 9 10 8 6 4 2

Printed in Italy

MIX
Paper from
responsible sources
FSC
www.fsc.org   FSC® C023419

To find out more about our authors and books visit www.bloomsbury.com and sign up for our newsletters

Mark SPERRING   Sophie CORRIGAN

HOT DOG

MUSTARD

TOMATO

BLOOMSBURY
CHILDREN'S BOOKS

LONDON OXFORD NEW YORK NEW DELHI SYDNEY

Once there was a **hot dog**
made of sausage and bread bun,
sitting on a hot dog stand
and feeling very glum.

PLANT-BASED
HOT DOGS
£2.99

TOMA

MUSTA

For everywhere around it,
on the lovely sandy beach
were real-life little puppy dogs,

with **heads**

and **tails**

and **feet**.

"I wish **I** was just like those dogs,"
that hot dog softly sighed.
"I'd sniff the air with my wet nose
and have **huge** puppy eyes.

I'd **fetch** a stick,

I'd **catch** a ball,

I'd even **chase my tail**.

But hot dogs can't do things like that –
my dream is doomed to fail."

But standing not too far away,
was someone who could help.
And when she heard the hot dog's wish
she flew down from the shelf.

"Fear not, my little hot dog,"
she told him with great cheer.
"For I'm the **Mustard Fairy** –
I bet you're glad I'm here!"

Then with a squirt of mustard,
and **another** squirt (or two . . .)
the fairy worked her magic,

and . . .

A hot dog's wish **came true!**

"Oh, **thank you!**"
said the hot dog,
with a bark of gratitude.
"Now I'm like those other dogs,
except I'm made of food!"

Then up he jumped and off he **raced**
to do things without fail . . .

Like **fetch** a stick,

and **catch** a ball,

and **chase his wagging tail!**

But up and down the sun-kissed beach,
the dogs all raised their snouts
to sniff the most **DELICIOUS** smell
that wafted all about . . .

Sniff-**Sniff**

they smelt a sausage

and,
Sniff-Sniff
a nice warm bun.

Then a **rumble** in their tummies
made those dogs all cry out . . .

Poor Hot Dog ran on little legs
as fast as he could go,
and headed for an ice-cream stand
whose owner was called Flo.

"Please help!"
begged little Hot Dog,
"for I've an AWFUL hunch,

that if those doggies catch me . . .
they'll want **ME**
for their lunch!"

Flo took one look at that anxious face
with its great big PUPPY eyes,
and knew she'd stop at nothing
to help this little guy.

So she reached behind the counter,
and said, "Don't you fret or weep,
for if those dogs are hungry, well . . .

HERE'S something they can eat!"

Then she launched some ice-pop lollies that **EXPLODED** on the ground,

and flung huge scoops of ice cream
to stop those charging hounds.

She **BLASTED** them
with strawberry sauce
and loads of
sprinkles too.

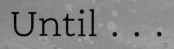
Until . . .

. . . those doggies ran away,
covered in **STICKY GOO!**

Hiding under a parasol
one little dog remained,
with sprinkles sticking to his back –
and **Hot Dog** was his name.

Flo felt her heart swell fit to burst
and as the pink sun set,
she asked that little sausage if . . .

He'd like to be **her pet!**

For a moment, one small creature
could NOT believe his ears,
and then those big round puppy eyes
filled up with **happy** tears.

"And to make life even sweeter,"
said Flo, **"here's what we'll do . . ."**

"We'll buy a
cotton-candy playmate
especially for you!"